The Amazing

Mr. Franklin

or The Boy Who Read Everything

To Ernie
—R.A.

Published by
PEACHTREE PUBLISHERS
1700 Chattahoochee Avenue
Atlanta, Georgia 30318-2112

www.peachtree-online.com

Text © 2004 by Ruth Ashby
Illustrations © 2004 by Michael Montgomery

10 9 8 7 6 5 4 3 2 1
First Edition

Book design by Loraine M. Joyner
Composition by Melanie Ives

Paintings created in oil on canvas
Text typeset in SWFTE International's Bronte; titles typeset in Luiz da Lomba's Theatre Antione

Printed in China

Library of Congress Cataloging-in-Publication Data
Ashby, Ruth.
  The amazing Mr. Franklin / written by Ruth Ashby.-- 1st ed.
    p. cm.
Summary: Introduces the life of inventor, statesman, and founding father Benjamin Franklin, whose love of books led him to establish the first public library in the American colonies.
  ISBN 1-56145-306-4
    1. Franklin, Benjamin, 1706-1790--Juvenile literature. 2. Statesmen--United States--Biography--Juvenile literature. 3. Scientists--United States--Biography--Juvenile literature. 4. Inventors--United States--Biography--Juvenile literature. 5. Printers--United States--Biography--Juvenile literature. [1. Franklin, Benjamin, 1706-1790. 2. Statesmen. 3. Scientists. 4. Inventors. 5. Printers.] I. Title.

E302.6.F8A78 2004
973.3'092--dc22
                            2003018740

The Amazing
Mr. Franklin
or The Boy Who Read Everything

Ruth Ashby

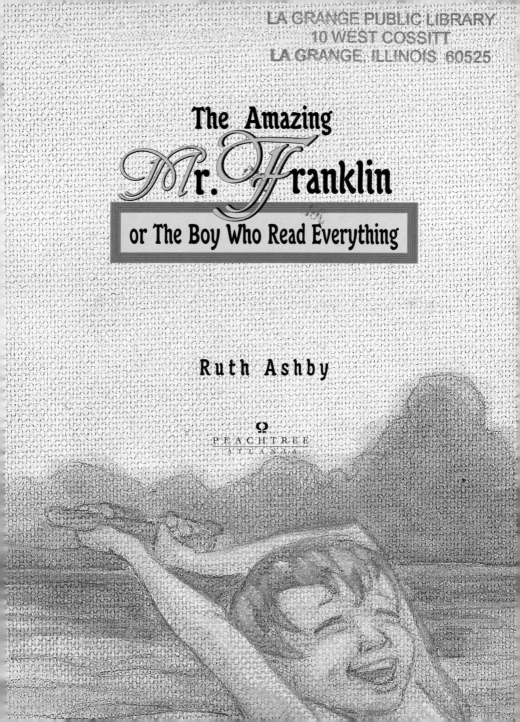

PEACHTREE
ATLANTA

Benjamin  Franklin

1749
Proposes future
University of Pennsylvania

1737
Becomes postmaster of Philadelphia

1732
Prints first edition of POOR RICHARD'S ALMANACK

1731
Forms the Library Company of Philadelphia with friends

1730
Marries Deborah Read

1729
Publishes first edition of the *Pennsylvania Gazette*

1728
Sets up his own printing shop

1723
Runs away to Philadelphia

1718
Becomes printer's apprentice
to his older brother James

1716
Goes to work in his father's
soap and candlemaking shop

1706
Born in Boston

1700   1710   1720   1730   1740

If you would not be forgotten, as soon as you are dead and rotten, either write things

1752
Performs famous kite and
key experiment

1757
Sent to London to discuss colonial
disputes with Parliament

1775
The Revolutionary War begins

1776
Advises Thomas Jefferson on writing the
Declaration of Independence
Sets sail for France

1778
Persuades France to recognize the United States
as a new nation and sign a Treaty of Alliance

1781
Helps negotiate peace as
Revolutionary War ends

1785-87
Returns home from France
Serves three terms as
president of Pennsylvania

1790
Dies on
April 17

1750   1760   1770   1780   1790

worth the reading, or do things worth the writing. *POOR RICHARD'S ALMANACK, 1738*

Acknowledgments

The author would like to thank

James N. Green and Cornelia S. King

at the Library Company of Philadelphia

for their invaluable help in researching this book,

and my editor, Lisa Banim, for giving me

the opportunity to write about Ben Franklin.

LIBRARY COMPANY OF PHILADELPHIA

Table of Contents

Chapter One
BOSTON BOY

Seventeen-year-old Ben Franklin was going to run away. He was tired of being an apprentice.

He didn't want to work for his older brother, James, anymore. It was time for him to strike out on his own and show the world what he could do.

It was a big decision. He would have to leave his family and friends—everybody and everything he knew—behind.

Ben had grown up in Boston, the son of a candle maker. His father Josiah had seventeen children, and Ben was the youngest boy. From the beginning, Josiah knew this son was special. Ben was bright and eager to learn. And he couldn't stay away from books. "I do not remember when I could not read," Ben wrote later.

Boston was just the right place for a curious boy. The bustling town on the sea had most of the books in the North American British colonies. It had the most people, too—12,000 in 1706, the year Ben was born. Boston had been founded in the 1630s by a group of strict Protestants, called Puritans. Puritans wanted everyone to be able to read the Bible. Every village in the new Massachusetts Bay Colony had its own school-house. As a result, nearly all the people in Boston could read, unlike most people in European cities at the time.

There were no public libraries, though. Anyone who wanted a book had to own it himself—or borrow it from someone else. Wealthy individuals had their own private libraries in religion, science, and history. Even Ben's father had a small home library.

There were no books written just for children, either. The first book Ben read was the Bible, when he was five. His next favorite was *The Pilgrim's Progress,* by John Bunyan. It was a symbolic story about a man named Christian who had lots of adventures as he struggled to become a good person. Ben liked the story because it was exciting. It also showed that people could improve themselves through their own efforts. That's what he wanted to do!

Even when he was young, Ben showed a flair for independent thinking. Once he was flying a kite near a local pond when he decided to take a swim. Grasping the string with both hands, he splashed into the water and lay on his back. The kite puffed out with the wind and pulled Ben across the pond. He was sailing!

Clearly, this inventive boy had special gifts. How should he put them to use?

Perhaps he could become a minister. In the early 1700s, clergymen were well-respected leaders of the community. When Ben was eight, his father sent him to Boston Latin School to study Greek and Latin. Ben was an excellent student. He shot straight up to the top of the class. But then Josiah pulled him out of school. Becoming a minister took many years and the training was very expensive. Ben would have to learn a trade, like most young boys his age.

At first Ben worked in the candle shop with his father. Candle making was hard work. Ben learned to boil beef and mutton fat to make tallow. He poured the tallow into molds and cut wicks for the candles. He ran errands, wrapped packages, and attended the shop. He was bored to death.

I'll run away to sea, Ben threatened. Josiah shuddered. That's exactly what Ben's eldest brother had done—and he had found a watery grave.

Josiah would do anything to keep Ben safe and on dry land. He took him around Boston to see all the craftsmen at their jobs: joiners, bricklayers, carpenters, shipwrights. Ben loved watching the men work with their hands. But none of these crafts seemed right for him. He would much rather read.

Ben had already run through his father's small collection of books. He had to buy his own. "All the little money that came into my hands, was ever laid out in books," Ben once said. He read history and biography and religion, books about famous battles and great men. But there were never enough books. How could there be, when there was so much to learn?

By the time he was a teenager, Ben discovered a smart way to save money for books. He could become a vegetarian! Beef and pork cost a lot more than potatoes and bread. So Ben stopped eating meat—and spent all the money he saved on books.

Finally Josiah hit upon a solution. Ben could become a printer! Printers had to be able to write and edit as well as set type and run off the printed sheets. It might be just the right job for a boy who loved words.

Luckily, Ben had a half-brother, James, who was opening a print shop in Boston. Josiah asked James if he would like an apprentice. James said he would. Then Josiah asked Ben if he would like to become that apprentice.

Yes!

Ben was so thankful to find a trade he might enjoy that he signed legal papers of indenture. The document said that James would teach Ben to become a printer. In return, Ben promised to work for James until he was twenty-one. That seemed a lifetime away to Ben. He was only twelve.

Ben knew right away that he'd made the right decision. Like candle making, printing was difficult and time-consuming work. But it was also fascinating. Not only did he get to set the type for books, newspapers, and pamphlets, he got to read all the articles, too!

As apprentice to a printer, Ben also met lots of other apprentices. Occasionally a bookseller's apprentice would smuggle him a book. Ben would read all night by candlelight and sneak the book back the next morning, before anyone discovered it was missing.

I bet *I* could be a writer, Ben told himself. He decided to practice.

First he tried his hand at poetry. But his father disapproved. Poets are generally beggars, Josiah said sharply.

Ben gave up on poetry. He found famous essays to imitate instead. He wrote them over again, using different words. He turned the ideas into rhyme, then back again to prose. Then he compared his version to the original essay.

It took a lot of effort. Ben was a perfectionist—he wanted to be a really *great* writer. "I was extremely ambitious," he admitted later.

Soon he had a chance to show off his new skills. Brother James decided to start a newspaper, one of the first in the colonies. He wanted it to be lively, full of Boston politics and gossip. James and his friends used pretend names like "Harry Meanwell" and "Homespun Jack" to write articles and editorials.

One morning James was delighted to discover a letter slipped under the print shop door. It was from a Mrs. Silence Dogood. Mrs. Dogood was a talkative widow with lots of strong opinions. She made fun of hoop skirts, bad poetry, and local politicians. Readers loved her, so Mrs. Dogood kept writing. All of Boston tried to guess her true identity.

Was Mrs. Dogood really a forty-year-old widow? No, she was a sixteen-year-old boy—Ben Franklin!

Excited and proud, Ben told his brother his secret. He expected praise. But James was annoyed. As far as he was concerned, Ben was getting a swelled head. The boy was only an apprentice, after all. How dare he trick his master?

The two brothers began to quarrel. James would order Ben to do something, and Ben would refuse. Often he was rude and saucy. Then, when James got really furious, he would beat him. That made Ben resent his brother even more.

Matters went from bad to worse. Then, one day, a crisis erupted. James was thrown into prison! His newspaper had printed an unfavorable story about the Massachusetts governor, who decided James deserved a lesson. While his brother was in jail, Ben took over the newspaper. He edited, printed, and published a whole issue by himself. At seventeen, he was the youngest editor in the colonies.

James was released, but soon he angered the governor again. This time, he was forbidden to publish the paper at all. He made a secret deal with Ben. Ben could run the paper—in public. In private, Ben would still be James's apprentice.

This wasn't going to work out. Ben didn't want to be under his brother's thumb for another five years. He wanted his freedom immediately. But he couldn't stay in Boston, where everyone knew him.

He would have to run away!

Where could he go? Ben wondered. Maybe New York. It was a growing city, with plenty of opportunities for a hardworking, ambitious boy. But Ben was penniless. Where would he find the money to pay for the journey?

There was only one answer. He would have to sell his most treasured possessions—his books!

Chapter Two
RUNAWAY

Quietly Ben prepared to run away. He had to work in secret. If James found out what he was up to, his plans would be ruined.

First, Ben sold a few of his precious books and gave the money to a friend named John Collins. Then Collins booked him a passage on a ship sailing out of Boston Harbor. On the evening of Wednesday, September 25, 1723, seventeen-year-old Benjamin Franklin sneaked onboard.

New York, ho!

The ship set sail in a fair wind. Ben's spirits were high. But then, after two days at sea, the breeze died down. The crew, with nothing else to do, went fishing. They hauled up a net full of cod and tossed them in a frying pan.

My, the fish smelled delicious!

But the young vegetarian was determined not to eat any. Killing fish was a kind of murder, Ben thought. What had the poor fish ever done to him to deserve death at his hands?

But when the fish were cut open, Ben saw that each larger fish had a smaller fish in its belly. Well, if you eat one another, Ben reasoned, I don't see why *I* may not eat *you!* So he forgot about his meatless diet and dug in.

Years later, Franklin drew a moral from his experience. Yes, humans are reasonable creatures, he wrote. They can find reasons for everything they want to do!

Eventually the ship arrived in New York Harbor. Now Ben was 300 miles from Boston, his brother, and the hated apprenticeship. He thought the worst part of his journey was over. He had no idea his troubles were just beginning!

The first challenge was to find a job. There was only one printer in New York, an older man named William Bradford. The morning he landed, Ben went to ask him for work.

Sorry, Bradford replied. I have no work available. Why not try my son Andrew in Philadelphia? Aquila Rose, his assistant, has just died, and he's looking for a new hand.

Philadelphia was another 100 miles away. But Ben had no choice. So off he set again, this time in a small boat with worn-out sails. As the frail vessel crossed New York Harbor, a huge storm came up. The wind wailed and the rain came down in torrents.

The rotten sails ripped apart—and the boat drifted off course!

Buffeted by the storm, the boat rocked violently in the heavy seas. No matter what Benjamin and the others did, they could not get it under control. Then an enormous wave hit the side of the boat. A Dutch passenger was hurled overboard.

The man thrashed about in the water. He was going to drown!

Quick as a flash, Ben reached overboard and grabbed the Dutchman by his hair. He pulled him over to the side of the boat. Then, with the others' help, he hauled him back onboard.

Ben Franklin had saved the man's life!

Exhausted, the Dutchman pulled a waterlogged book out of his pocket and asked Ben to dry it for him. Then he fell asleep.

Ben glanced at the book. It was his old friend *The Pilgrim's Progress!* He flipped through it and looked at the pictures. There was Christian, traveling through the dangerous Valley of the Shadow of Death. Dragons and hobgoblins threatened him on either side. Now Ben, too, was having a perilous adventure. He hoped that, like Christian, he would reach his goal safely. Maybe finding his favorite book was a good sign.

The boat drifted out of New York Harbor and over to the shores of Long Island. As they neared the beach, the passengers could see breakers pounding the sand. People hailed them from the beach.

Ben waved back and cupped his hands around his mouth. Please rescue us! he called out.

But no one came. The waves were too high and the coming night too dark for rescuers to risk the trip. Everyone on board knew the boat would be smashed in the surf if they tried to make a landing.

So Ben and his companions spent a miserable night on the open sea. In the salt spray, they were nearly as wet and cold as the rescued Dutchman. All they had on board to eat or drink was a bottle of rum. They passed it around, taking sips to warm their stomachs.

In the morning the men managed to rig the ripped sails. Slowly they made their way over to New Jersey and came ashore at the town of Perth Amboy. They had been on the water for thirty hours.

Ben was hungry and feverish. He stumbled into an inn and threw himself into bed. But before going to sleep, he drank a jug of cold water. He had read in one of his books that drinking water was good for a fever.

Sure enough, when Ben awoke the next morning he felt much better. It was a good thing he had recovered from his illness, because now he had to walk fifty miles across New Jersey to the Delaware River. From there he could get a boat downstream to Philadelphia.

It rained all day. By the time Ben finally got to an inn, he was soaked all the way through. The innkeeper gave him a funny look.

Who are you? he asked suspiciously. Where do you come from? Where are you going?

Ben realized that the innkeeper thought he was a runaway servant. He finished his meal quickly and went to bed.

He was beginning to wish he'd never left home.

Then Ben's luck turned. The next night he stayed with a man named Mr. Browne, who was delighted to find that this grubby teenager loved books as much as he did. They talked for hours, and ended up being friends for life.

By the next evening Ben had reached the Delaware River. As he walked along the riverfront, he saw a boat going to Philadelphia. He decided to hitch a ride. When they approached Philadelphia, it was still dark. No one on the boat could spot the city. At almost midnight, they rowed to shore and made a fire. Ben spent the night shivering in the cool October air.

Morning dawned at last. The group paddled back out onto the river, the fog lifted—and there they saw it: Philadelphia, City of Brotherly Love. This place would be Ben's home for most of the next sixty-seven years.

They landed at Market Street. Years later, Ben remembered the strange picture he must have presented. "I was dirty from my journey," he wrote. "My pockets were stuffed out with shirts and stockings…I was fatigued with traveling, rowing, and want of rest." And above all, "I was very hungry."

And so, filthy and famished, young Benjamin Franklin set out to make his fortune.

Chapter Three
READY, SET, PRINT

Ben walked down Market Street and looked around. Philadelphia was so different from Boston! Instead of the wooden houses he was used to, red brick buildings lined the streets. Instead of winding and curving like the streets of Boston, the roads here were straight and orderly. And many of the people he heard on the streets were not speaking English.

William Penn had founded the city just fifty years before. He was an English Quaker who wanted to create a place where people from different backgrounds and religions could live and work together. Penn had established a government based on the principles of religious freedom, trial by jury, and voting for representatives. He named his city Philadelphia, "City of Brotherly Love." People from many places across the ocean—Germany, England, Scotland, Wales, and Ireland—flocked to the new city.

Philadelphia was just part of Pennsylvania, the large area of land that British King Charles II had granted Penn in 1681. The Penn family governed Pennsylvania (the name means "Penn's woods") until the American Revolution. At the time when Ben Franklin arrived in Philadelphia, there were twelve English colonies along the east coast of North America: Massachusetts, Vermont, Rhode Island, Connecticut, New York, Pennsylvania, Delaware, Maryland, Virginia, North Carolina, and South Carolina.

Ben would have plenty of time to find out about his adopted colony. But first, he had to find something to eat. He asked directions to the nearest bakery.

Have you any biscuits? he asked the baker.

No, came the brief reply.

Ben tried again. How about a three-penny loaf, then?

We have none such, the baker said firmly.

Ben was growing desperate. Then I'll take three pennyworth of anything you have, he said.

To his delight, he received not one, but three large, puffy rolls. He stuffed two of them into his pockets and one into his mouth.

He continued his stroll down Market Street. A girl about his age leaned out of a doorway and stifled a giggle. The tall young man with the roll in his mouth looked so ridiculous!

Ben pulled the two rolls from his pocket and gave them to a mother and child who had traveled with him on the boat. Then he fell in behind a group of clean, neatly dressed people. They were all walking in the same direction.

After a while, Ben realized that the people were Quakers, on their way to Sunday Meeting. Curious, he followed them into the meetinghouse and sat on one of the hard wooden pews. He was surprised when no one said anything. In Quaker services, no preacher stands up to give a sermon. Members of the congregation are free to speak when the spirit moves them.

Ben was so tired, and the meeting was so quiet, that he soon dozed off. The Quakers kindly let him sleep until the meeting was over.

That night Ben found a bed at a local lodging house. On Monday morning, he tried to clean up as best he could. Then he set off for Andrew Bradford's print shop.

He had arrived a few days too late. Bradford had already hired another hand to replace Aquila Rose.

There was, however, a new printer in town. Perhaps, Bradford suggested, Franklin might want to try him?

Ben found the new printer hard at work, composing a poem in memory of the same Aquila Rose. Samuel Keimer bent over the type case, his long straggly beard brushing the table. He had a unique way of writing. Instead of setting the poem down with pen and paper first, he placed the letters for each line into the type case as he composed it—the words came right out of his head and went straight into the press!

Franklin looked around at the old, broken-down press and small stock of type. He could tell the shop was struggling. Keimer, he decided, was definitely an odd fish.

But luckily, the printer did need an assistant. Ben had found himself a job! Within a few days, he had a place to live as well. It was at the home of John Read, next to Keimer's shop on Market Street. Read's daughter Deborah was the very same young lady who had laughed at Ben the morning he came into town.

Luckily, the chest with his clothes and books had finally arrived from Boston. Ben was once again scrubbed and well dressed. Even Miss Read had to agree that he made a respectable appearance.

Now it was time for Ben to get to work.

Printing was a nearly 300-year-old profession in 1723. Yet it had not changed much since the 1440s, when German printer Johannes Gutenberg had invented the wooden press and movable type. "Movable type" means that each metal letter of the alphabet can be moved and used more than once. In a print shop, metal letters were kept in trays called cases. The upper sections, or upper cases, held the capital letters. The lower cases held the small letters. Today, capital letters are still called "upper case," while small letters are called "lower case."

Typesetters, or compositors, would set the type on a composing stick. There they put letters into words and words into sentences. The words had to be set upside down and backwards, so that their reverse image on paper would be right side up and forward. It took a lot of skill to be able to compose. Compositors were prized for their speed and accuracy. Not surprisingly, Ben was an exceptionally good compositor.

Once set, the lines of type would be locked into a metal frame and the frame placed on the printing press. The printer inked the type with two leather balls. Then he slid the type under the press, or platen. Pulling a handle called the devil's tail, he pressed the dampened paper against the inked type. When he removed the printed paper, he hung it on a clothesline, called a fly, to dry. The papers were known as "flyers."

Operating a printing press took strength and agility. Young Ben was also a quick, tireless printer.

Two printers working a ten-hour day could turn out almost 2,000 sheets of paper. This did not include the time it took to compose the type. In the summer, a working day could run as long as twelve or fourteen hours, or as long as daylight lasted. Printing houses were much more productive in the summer than in the winter. No one wanted to compose by the flickering light of a candle. It led to too many mistakes.

What did a colonial print shop print? Any and all paper products the community needed. The government hired printers to print paper money, speeches, laws, land deeds, and other documents. Churches hired them to print sermons, hymns, and church announcements. For the community at large, the press printed books, pamphlets, broadsides, newspapers, almanacs, prayer books, advertisements, lottery tickets, invitations, schoolbooks, and blank legal forms. A colonial print shop was a bookstore, stationery store, and home entertainment center rolled into one!

When Ben arrived in Philadelphia, the town already had two print shops. To someone as ambitious as Ben, they meant competition. Someday, Ben wanted to have his own print shop and become the best printer in Philadelphia. He sized up his rivals. Although Keimer was a good compositor—and a sometime poet—he knew nothing of presswork. Bradford, on the other hand, did not have the writing skills necessary for the job. He was "very illiterate," Ben judged.

It looked as though Philadelphia could use someone with Benjamin Franklin's gifts.

As he was to do all his life, Ben immediately made friends in his new town. At age seventeen, Ben was an attractive young man. Nearly six feet tall with a frank, open face, he attracted people with his charm and chattiness. He sought out other young men who were "lovers of reading." He worked hard, saved money, and tried to forget about his old life in Boston.

But he couldn't escape that easily. Six months after he arrived in Philadelphia, his past caught up with him.

Ben had a brother-in-law, Robert Homes, who was captain of a trading ship. Homes heard Ben was in Philadelphia and sent him a letter. He assured Ben that if he returned to Boston, his friends and family would forgive him. Ben immediately wrote back, explaining his reasons for leaving. He had no intention of returning, he said.

Homes happened to open the letter in the company of Sir William Keith, the governor of Pennsylvania. Keith was amazed that such a young man could write so well. Surely such talent should be encouraged!

One day Ben Franklin and Samuel Keimer were working together near the window of Keimer's shop. A very well dressed man walked over from across the street—and knocked at the shop door. It was Governor Keith!

Keimer became very excited. Perhaps the governor had come to see him on important business!

He was shocked when the governor asked to speak to Ben instead. And he was even more put out when such a distinguished man invited the boy to a meeting! Would Mr. Franklin care to accompany him to a nearby tavern for a friendly glass and a chat? the governor asked. Surprised, Ben agreed. As for Keimer, Ben wrote later, he "stared like a pig poisoned."

After some small talk, Keith laid out his proposal. He promised Ben lots of government business if Ben would set up his own print shop. Keith was sure that Ben's father would lend him the money to pay for it. And to convince Josiah Franklin that the offer was sincere, the governor would write Ben a letter of recommendation.

So seven months after Ben ran away from home, he

returned to Boston triumphant, with £5 silver in his pocket. Decked out in a brand-new suit and watch, he looked very different from the young man who had sneaked on board the ship in the Boston harbor. His parents, who hadn't known whether Ben was alive or dead, were very happy to see him.

His brother James, though, was not pleased at all. Ben visited the print shop in all his finery and strutted in front of the other workers, boasting about his success in Philadelphia. They, of course, were very impressed. But James felt insulted.

Ben was disappointed when his father refused to give him the funds to set up his own business. Josiah Franklin was a thoughtful and practical man. He figured that Ben was still a boy. How could the governor think that a seventeen-year-old had the experience or wisdom to manage his own business? Keith might have good intentions, Josiah decided, but he could not have much common sense.

Josiah told Ben that he should continue to work hard and save his earnings. Then, when Ben was twenty-one, Josiah would provide his son with the rest of the money to open his shop.

Ben had to be content with this promise. Armed with his parents' love and blessings, he returned to

Philadelphia. His old friend James Collins also came with him, eager to seek his own fortune.

Never mind, Governor Keith told Ben when he heard of Josiah Franklin's decision. Since he will not set you up, I will do it myself.

Ben was excited. Soon he would have just what he'd always wanted—a print shop of his own!

Chapter Four
A BOLD SCHEME

Ben listened happily as Governor Keith discussed his plans for the new printing business.

"Give me a list of the things you need from England," Keith said, "and I will send for them. You shall repay me when you are able. I am resolved to have a good printer here in Philadelphia, and I am sure you must succeed."

Ben thought hard. He would need a wooden printing press, of course. Two composing sticks, eight cases, six galleys (metal frames to hold type), and various other pieces of equipment. And, most important, 1,200 pounds of metal type, in eight sizes.

Altogether, the equipment would cost £100 sterling, a good deal of money in those days.

No problem, Governor Keith said. Perhaps Ben would like to go to England himself? That way he could choose his own type and make the business contacts he would need in London.

England? Ben would love to go!

In 1724, many colonists dreamed of visiting the mother country. But pirates and the constant wars in Europe made the voyage so dangerous that only one ship traveled between Philadelphia and London in a whole year. Ben would have many months to wait until the next ship set sail.

In the meantime, he continued to work for Samuel Keimer. The older man was strange, no doubt about it. But Ben found it amusing to debate him, especially about religion. Keimer belonged to an unusual religious group that worshipped on Saturday, instead of Sunday. Men wore their beards long and untrimmed. He proposed that Ben, too, join his group and grow a beard. Ben agreed, on condition that Keimer become a vegetarian. After his fish feast on shipboard, Ben had stopped being a full-time vegetarian. Yet he still returned to a meatless diet now and then to save money.

Now he and Keimer agreed not to eat fish, meat, or fowl for three months. Ben was proud of all the money he saved on his diet. But Keimer, a "great glutton," was going crazy. They agreed to break their fast with a big dinner. But when the roast pig was delivered, Keimer ate it all himself before the other guests arrived!

Ben wasn't getting along with his friend James Collins, the young man who had traveled with him from Boston, at all. They had been friends since childhood, and read many books together. But now Ben discovered to his dismay that Collins had become a drunkard. Because of his drinking, he couldn't hold down a job in Philadelphia. Instead, he kept borrowing money from his friend. Ben became more and more angry, until finally his fury erupted.

One day, while they were boating on the Delaware River with some other friends, Collins refused to take his turn at the oars. "I will be rowed home," he declared grandly.

"We will not row you," Ben snapped.

"You must," Collins said, "or you must stay all night on the water."

The other passengers, fearing a fight, said they would row instead. But Ben was too annoyed to let Collins have his way. Swearing that he would make Ben row in his place, Collins stood up in the rocking boat. Ben's patience snapped. He lifted Collins up into the air—and pitched him headfirst into the river!

Every time Collins swam near, the rowers pulled the

boat out of his reach. Still, he would not give in. Finally, when Ben saw that Collins was getting tired, they let him back on board. But the friendship was over. A few months later, Collins left to become a tutor in the West Indies. Collins never paid back the money he owed Ben, and Ben never heard from his childhood friend again.

Franklin had other friends, "lovers of reading" with whom he wrote and recited poetry. The best of the poets, James Ralph, decided to go to London with Ben. Ben thought it was for business reasons. Only later did he discover that Ralph wanted to escape his wife's relatives—and his wife.

By now Ben was involved in his own romance. He and Deborah Read had grown quite fond of each other and wanted to get married. But they were both still very young, only eighteen. Deborah's mother thought they should wait until Ben got back from London. So Deborah and Ben exchanged many promises, and agreed to wait.

Finally the great day arrived. Ben was eager to set off for London. All he needed were the letters of introduction and credit from Governor Keith. Before his departure, Ben called at the governor's house to pick up the letters. They were not ready. But the governor's secretary promised they would be delivered at New Castle before the ship sailed. At New Castle, however, Ben was told that the letters would be sent on board in a general mailbag. Ben boarded the ship, a little puzzled.

Why had Governor Keith not prepared the letters?

The voyage was uneventful. Ben and James Ralph made several new acquaintances, including an extremely pleasant Quaker merchant named Mr. Denham.

Finally, as the ship neared London, the ship's captain let Ben examine the bag of letters. Strangely, he found none with his name on it. Where were the letters the governor had promised him?

Worried, Ben told Mr. Denham about his dilemma. The merchant looked grave. Everyone knows Governor Keith is an undependable man, he said. He has a very a bad habit of making promises he can never keep.

There is no doubt about it, said Mr. Denham. You will not get letters of recommendation, money, or anything else from such a man.

Ben had been fooled!

The ship arrived in London on Christmas Eve, 1724. Ben looked around him in awe. London was the largest city in Europe, home to nearly 700,000 people.

What was he going to do? He was alone in the largest city in the world, with no money, no work—and no way to get home!

Chapter Five
DOWN — BUT NOT OUT

Yes, Ben was penniless. But luckily he had the skills to make a living. He was able to find work immediately at a famous printing house named Palmer's. He and Ralph found cheap lodgings. Then they set out to have fun.

All London was a playground for the two young men. They went to the theater and other amusements. Franklin was having such a good time that he forgot all about poor Deborah Read. He wrote her only once, to tell her he would not be coming back to Philadelphia any time soon.

For his part, Ralph had no intention of returning to his wife and child. However, he was unable to obtain steady work, and Ben had to help him out. Finally they quarreled and parted company.

Ben got a better job at an even larger printing house. As soon as the foreman discovered what a good compositor he was, he was given all the rush jobs, which were generally better paid. Most of Ben's fellow workers got through the day by drinking pint after pint of watered-down beer. Ben, though, refused to cloud his brain. He became known as the Water American.

Ben also hungered for books. Although London had no lending libraries, for a while Ben had the good fortune to lodge next to a bookseller. For a low fee, he was permitted to borrow second-hand books, read them, and return them promptly. He made as much use of the privilege as he could.

By the time Ben had been in London for about a year and a half, he started to get restless. It was then that his shipboard friend Thomas Denham approached him with an intriguing offer.

Denham was someone Ben felt he could truly trust and admire. Years before, the Quaker merchant had left London deeply in debt and made a fortune in America. When he returned to London, he treated all his debtors to a grand feast. Under each of their plates, they found the money he owed them—plus interest!

Now Denham was going back to Philadelphia to

open a store. Would Ben like to become his clerk? he asked.

Yes! Ben jumped at the chance. He was tired of London and longed to see America once more.

So in July 1726, Franklin once again set sail across the Atlantic.

The voyage lasted three long months, giving Ben plenty of time to think. Thanks in part to all the books he had read, he was very interested in science. Why not use the extra hours to indulge his scientific curiosity?

When Ben found tiny crabs nested in some seaweed, he guessed that perhaps the seaweed had hatched the crabs. In order to test his theory, he hauled in some more seaweed, placed it in a bucket of salt water, and waited to see what happened. Unfortunately, the seaweed died. Ben never did figure out that plants could not give birth to animals! Later in the voyage, he performed a more successful scientific procedure. He used a lunar eclipse to calculate the distance from London.

He also took some time to take stock of his life. In the last few years, Ben felt that he had wasted too much time, spent too much money, and let down some of his friends, especially Deborah Read. He resolved to do better.

From now on, he would:
1. Save money
2. Tell the truth
3. Work hard
4. Speak ill of no man

It was the first of many plans Benjamin Franklin made for self-improvement during his life.

He arrived back in Philadelphia on October 11, and went to work in Denham's store. With his friendliness and charm, he was a natural salesman. But then tragedy struck. Just a few months after they got home, Denham fell sick and died. Ben's hopes of becoming a successful merchant died, too. He had no choice but to return to Samuel Keimer's shop as a manager.

Ben was very useful to Keimer. When they ran out of type, Ben figured out a way to cast new type using lead molds. He was the first American to do so. He also made ink, acted as the "warehouse man," and, in short, became a jack-of-all-trades. He even invented a special copperplate press to print New Jersey paper money. In his spare time, Ben trained four apprentices. Still, he felt dissatisfied. He longed to be working for himself.

Then there was Deborah Read. Ben had completely ignored her while in London. Not knowing what had become of him, Deborah had married a ne'er-do-well pottery maker named John Rogers. When Deborah heard rumors that Rogers also had a wife in England, she moved back in with her mother. Now her husband had taken off for the West Indies. Poor Deborah was left alone, neither married nor free. Ben was ashamed of himself when he saw her.

But Ben would not be down for long. He learned that the father of Hugh Meredith, one of Keimer's apprentices, wanted to set his son up in his own printing business. Meredith and Ben formed a partnership. Meredith would provide the money, Ben the expertise. They ordered a press and equipment from England. As soon as the shipment arrived, both young men bid farewell to Keimer.

At age twenty-two, Ben Franklin was his own boss at last.

Chapter Six
MOST LIKELY TO SUCCEED

The firm of Franklin and Meredith opened for business in a new office on Market Street. Their first customer walked in almost immediately. The money they earned that day, Ben remembered afterward, gave him more pleasure than any he made later.

There were already two successful printers in Philadelphia. How was Franklin to compete?

First, he would work harder than anyone else. When a friend got him an important job printing a history of the Quakers, Ben pushed himself to complete four pages a day. Often he finished later than eleven o'clock at night. One evening when a frame broke and ruined two pages, he stayed up most of the night to compose them again.

Second, he made sure that everyone *knew* how hard he was working. One nearby doctor reported to his friends that he saw young Franklin at his press before the neighbors got out of bed—and still at work when he got home from his last patient late at night.

Franklin thought of himself as a walking advertisement for his business. He wanted not only to be, but also to *look* the part of the successful tradesman. He dressed plainly; he didn't go fishing or shooting. And he made sure that he was never seen wasting time. Ben even pushed his paper up Market Street on a wheelbarrow, knowing that his neighbors were taking note of his hard efforts. A book was the only thing that could tempt him from work—but that didn't matter, because he always read in private, where no one could see him.

Unfortunately, Ben could not count on his new partner to hold up his end of the bargain. Meredith was a poor worker and bad compositor. Besides, he drank too much. With the help of some friends, Franklin bought Meredith's part of the business. On July 14, 1730, the partnership was broken. Meredith became a farmer in the Carolinas, and the two remained friends. But now Franklin was on his own.

Ben went back to his ambitious plan for self-improvement. How could he be as good a businessman—and as good a person—as possible? "I wished to live without committing any faults at any time," he wrote in his *Autobiography* many years later.

In other words, Ben wanted to be perfect!

He made up a list of thirteen virtues he wanted to have. Then he wrote them all down in a little book. Each week he decided to concentrate on one of the virtues. If he made a mistake, he would put a black mark on that day.

Soon his little book was full of black marks. Becoming perfect was much harder than he thought! "I was surprised to find myself so much fuller of faults than I had imagined," Ben admitted. Some virtues, like working hard and keeping clean, came to him naturally. Some he found much more difficult to develop.

Being orderly, for instance. Surprisingly, Franklin was a sloppy man. He had trouble keeping papers and other things neat and in the right places. Instead, he relied on his very good memory to remember where things were and what he had to do.

He compared himself to a man who wanted his axe sharpened and polished so that the whole surface shone brightly. A blacksmith agreed to hold the blade to the stone if the man turned the wheel. After a long time, the man grew tired and begged the blacksmith to stop. "But the axe is not shiny enough," the blacksmith replied. "I think I like a speckled axe best," the exhausted man decided.

In the same way, Franklin said, people may have to accept their own "speckled," far-from-perfect selves. Besides, he reasoned, every man should allow himself a few faults. If he did not, he would lose all his friends. Nobody likes a goody-goody!

Nonetheless, Franklin kept his notebook faithfully for many years. If he couldn't be perfect, he could still try!

Two months after he broke off with Meredith, Franklin entered into another partnership. He got married.

For a long time, Ben didn't know what to do about Deborah Read. No one knew whether her husband was alive or dead. If Rogers was alive, then Deborah would be breaking the law by marrying again. If he was dead, then Franklin would inherit his debts if he married her. It seemed to be a problem with no solution. So Ben tried courting other women. But for one reason or another, nothing worked out. He came back to Deborah.

Even though Ben had treated her badly, Deborah's family was still friendly. And so was she. On September 1, 1730, Ben and Deborah solved their problem by moving in with each other. Deborah began to call herself 'Mrs. Franklin." They had entered into what is called a "common law marriage," legal in the colonies. It lasted until Deborah's death, forty-four years later. "She proved a good and faithful helpmate," Franklin wrote. Most important, he said, they always tried to make each other happy.

Debby, as Ben called her, was smart and lively and loved her husband very much. Once he compared her to a round mug he had seen. It was molded in the shape of a "fat, jolly dame, clean and tidy, with a neat blue and white calico gown on, good-natured and lovely."

Deborah did not share her husband's intellectual interests. Like most women of the time, she was not very well educated. Her spelling was not good. "I have to tell you sum thing of my self," she once wrote Franklin. "What I believe you wold not beleve of me oney I tell you my seleve. I have bin to a play with sister."

One of the reasons Ben and Debby were such a good match was because Debby was as hard a worker as her husband. She helped him by tending shop, folding and stitching pamphlets, and buying old linen rags to make paper. The two of them opened a general store in the print shop that sold, among other things, legal forms, chocolate, cheese, codfish, tea, coffee, slates, ink, sealing wax, soap, and good parchment paper.

They also sold books. In 1730, there were no book-sellers in Philadelphia. The largest bookseller in the colonies was Isaiah Thomas of Worcester, Massa-chusetts, who had published nearly a thousand titles. Ben started small, with books he knew would sell, pri-marily psalms and hymnbooks. He published and sold works by friends, such as Latin translations or almanacs. He was the first American to publish a novel: Samuel Richardson's *Pamela,* a runaway bestseller in England. Like any good businessman, he wanted to make a profit.

He also imported books from England to sell, such as volumes of poetry by well-known English authors. Ordinarily Franklin read mostly nonfiction. But he also enjoyed poetry.

By 1744, Ben was selling a catalog of 600 volumes in law, religion, history, literature, science and mathemat-ics. Franklin was the biggest bookseller south of Boston. Best of all, he had the chance to read most of the books himself.

He was writing a lot, too—because by then, Ben owned his own newspaper.

Chapter Seven
A Not-So-Secret Club

Ben's newspaper, the *Pennsylvania Gazette,* did not start off as his own business. It was founded by his old employer Samuel Keimer. But Keimer ran the business so badly that he sold the *Gazette* to Franklin in October 1729, and ran off to Barbados.

Franklin was determined to make a success of his new venture. "There are many who have long desired to see a good newspaper in Pennsylvania," he said in his first letter to readers. The *Pennsylvania Gazette* was going to fill that need. Franklin filled the paper with local and foreign news, poems, jokes, advertisements, letters, essays from other journals, entertainment, and general information. He hoped his newspaper would reach the whole Pennsylvania community. He printed notices in Welsh for the Welsh settlers and in German for the Germans.

Much of the paper he wrote himself. Finally he could print all the silly jokes he heard and opinions he held. As he had done in the Silence Dogood papers, Ben wrote editorials under pen names. "Anthony Afterwit" complained about a wife who spent too much money. "Alice Addertongue" gossiped about her neighbors.

Sometimes Franklin was criticized for the wide array of opinions he allowed in the *Gazette*. He believed that public discussion was the role of a newspaper. In his famous "Apology for Printers," he stated his views as a publisher. People's opinions, he said, are "almost as various as their faces." Opposing views deserved to be aired. He himself didn't have to agree with everything he printed. If he did, "the world would afterwards have nothing to read but what happened to be the opinions of printers."

However, Ben refused to print anything he thought was hurtful or false. Once a customer urged him to publish such an article. Franklin refused, then thought about the money he would lose if he turned down paying customers. Did he dare refuse work in order to stand up for a principle? He decided to test himself.

As he later recounted in the *Gazette,* he had nothing

but bread and water for supper and spent the night on the floor, wrapped in his coat. The next morning he breakfasted on bread and water again. He felt fine. Apparently he could live on very little if he had to! No matter what happened, he would never have to lower himself for money.

Franklin also knew that it was impossible to satisfy everyone. To illustrate his point, he told a fable. A man, a boy, and a horse were traveling along a road. First the boy rode the horse. Everyone who went by criticized him for making his old father walk. Then the man rode the horse. They scolded him for tiring out his young son. Then no one rode the horse. What foolish people, the passersby said. The man and boy were walking when they could be riding in comfort!

Finally, the travelers made a drastic decision. "My son," the old man said. "It grieves me much that we cannot please all these people. Let us throw the [horse] over the next bridge, and be no farther troubled with him."

The moral? You can't please all of the people all of the time!

Ben Franklin was a busy man about town—printer, newspaperman, husband, shopkeeper. He had one more role—club member. In 1727 he founded a club for other young working men like himself. Some people called it the Leather Apron Club, because many of the members wore leather aprons at their jobs. But its official name was the Junto, which means "meeting" in Spanish. There were twelve members in all—a glassmaker, a scrivener (copyist), a cobbler, a cabinetmaker, a merchant's clerk, a silversmith, a shoemaker, a surveyor, and a handful of printers. What they all had in common was a desire for knowledge and an interest in self-improvement.

The club had been Franklin's idea from the beginning, of course. He was inspired by reading about different societies in Britain and New England. The Junto reflected his belief that people could join together to help themselves and their communities.

New members had to put their hands over their hearts and answer four questions.

Q: Do you have any disrespect for any current member?
A: No

Q: Do you love mankind in general no matter what their religion or profession?
A: Yes

Q: Do you feel people should ever be punished because of their opinions or religion?
A: No

Q: Do you love truth for its own sake?
A: Yes

Every Friday evening the group met in a tavern for friendly conversation. They discussed many different topics: What causes human happiness? What is wisdom? Is it possible for anyone to attain perfection? If a king takes away his subject's rights, can the subject resist?

Sometimes the topics were more concrete: How can we judge good writing? Franklin answered this one himself. Good writing, he said, should be "smooth, clear, and short."

And sometimes the questions reflected Franklin's scientific interests: Why does dew form on the outside of a cold mug? How can a smoky chimney be cured?

The club had a more practical side, too. Its members helped each other achieve their goals. Franklin understood that teamwork was the key to success. "He that drinks his cider alone, let him catch his horse alone," he used to say.

He made up a list of ways members could aid each other. "Is there any man whose friendship you want and which the Junto or any of them can procure [get] for you?" "In what manner can the Junto or any of them assist you in any of your honorable designs?" "Has anybody attacked your reputation lately, and what can the Junto do toward securing it?"

There were also ways the Junto could aid the community. "Have you lately observed any encroachments on [interference with] the just liberties of the people?" "Have you lately observed any defect [flaw] in the laws of your country of which it would be proper to move the legislature for an amendment?" "Hath any deserving stranger arrived in town since last meeting that you heard of? And what have you heard of his character or merits?"

Even though the Junto was supposed to be a secret society, its reputation grew. So many people wanted to join that soon there were four or five spin-off clubs. The Junto lasted thirty years. Franklin never got tired of it. "I love company, chat, a laugh, a glass, and even a song," he admitted.

Members of the Junto were interested in a wide range of topics. But whenever they had a disagreement or wanted to find out more about a particular subject, they had few places to turn for answers. Not only was there no Internet or TV—there were no public libraries and very little printed matter was available to them. They needed more books.

Franklin, in particular, needed more books. As his biographer Carl van Doren said, "there were books in his private life, books in his business, books in his friendship." Ben didn't just read books; he devoured them. As soon as he put one down, he was ready for the next.

What he needed was a book express service, straight from London, the book capital of the world, to his doorstep in Philadelphia. And how was he going to manage something like that?

Chapter Eight
BOOKS, BOOKS, AND MORE BOOKS

At first Ben came up with a simple solution to the problem of too few books. Why couldn't Junto members all pool their books into a common library?

By now, the club was renting a room for its weekly meetings. Each member brought in whatever books he could spare. Soon one end of the room was filled with bookshelves. But there were two problems. First, there weren't as many books as they had expected. Second, members worried that their own personal books would be ruined by constant handling. So after a year, all of them took their books home again.

So Franklin proposed Solution Number Two: A library!

Why not start a library that Junto members and other people could join? It would be a subscription library, with members paying dues.

Franklin suggested the idea to his friends. They were excited. So he drew up a charter for the "Library Company of Philadelphia." Members would hand over forty shillings at first. Then every year after that, they would pay another ten shillings to cover the cost of new books.

Franklin wrote the motto for the library: *Communiter Bona profundere Deum est* (To pour forth benefits for the common good is divine). Silversmith Phillip Syng designed the seal. It pictured two open books with water streaming between them. The water flowed into one large urn and then into many urns beneath.

Now all Ben had to do was find fifty people who wanted to join. This proved harder than he thought. To begin with, Philadelphia had few serious readers. And most of them did not have a great deal of money.

So Franklin had to sell his idea. At first he presented the library as a brainstorm of his own.

How would you like to join my library? he would ask a prospective customer.

The man would mull it over. Ben Franklin is founding a library? he would think suspiciously. But why? And how is *he* going to benefit?

So Ben changed his approach. Even though the library was really his idea, he wouldn't take credit for it.

My friends and I are starting a library, he would begin. Perhaps, as a lover of reading, you would like to join?

This time, customers were flattered—and much more interested.

In four months the Library Company had its fifty members. Now it needed some books. Franklin asked the best scholar in Pennsylvania, James Logan, for some advice. Logan, who could read Greek, Latin, Hebrew, French, and Italian, had hundreds of volumes in his own library. He had plenty of suggestions for Ben and his friends.

The library members settled on a final list of forty-five books. It included eight works on history, nine on science, eight on politics, and various other reference works. In March 1732, they sent the list off to Peter Collinson, a London merchant who would purchase the books for them. Then they sat back to wait for the shipment.

One month, two months, four months slipped by. The excitement grew. When would the books arrive? The boxes finally came in October. Members tore into them eagerly.

They rented a room to house the new collection. Louis Timothée, a printer who worked in Franklin's shop, was their first librarian. He opened the room from two to three o'clock on Wednesday afternoons and from ten to four on Saturdays. What Franklin called the "Mother of all the North American Subscription Libraries" was open for business.

At first only subscribers could take out books. But any "civil gentleman" could sit in the library and read. Borrowers could take out just one book at a time. To make sure they would bring the book back, they had to leave an IOU note for the cost of the book.

Gifts began pouring in. Many members of the Library Company contributed their own books. Franklin gave a reprint of the Magna Carta. Proprietor Thomas Penn sent a print of an orrery, which they framed and hung in a place of honor. The orrery, invented in 1700, is a mechanical model of the solar system.

In 1741, the Library Company printed its first catalog of books. It included nearly 400 volumes. The collection was about one-third history, including geography and travel books. Literature and science made up about 20 percent each. Religion made up only 10 percent. Earlier libraries at the colleges of Harvard and Yale, which educated young men to become ministers, contained mostly religious books.

There were more works by English philosopher John

Locke than any other single author. Locke was a strong supporter of individual liberty. In his essays, he said that all people have the right to "life, liberty, and estate [property]." If a government took away the people's rights, it should be overthrown. In other words, people had the right to revolt! Locke had a strong influence on Franklin and the other leaders of the American Revolution.

The Library Company is considered the first public library in the colonies. Although it was supported by private money, it was open to the general public. By 1741, it had nearly seventy members. The model was copied throughout the Thirteen Colonies. Libraries opened in New York, in Charleston, South Carolina, and in Newport, Rhode Island. By the time of the Revolutionary War, there were about seventy subscription libraries in all the colonies.

Ben Franklin was delighted. "Reading became fashionable," he wrote. "Our people having no public amusements to divert their attention from study became better acquainted with books, and in a few years were observed by strangers to be better instructed and more intelligent than people of the same rank generally are in other countries."

In the coming years, Franklin would found many

other Philadelphia institutions. All his life he believed in public service. "The good men may do separately is small compared with what they may do [together]," he used to say. First he would read a paper to the Junto, explaining a problem that needed fixing. Then he would publish his ideas in his newspaper. With his friends' help, he organized the first Philadelphia fire brigade and the first organization of night watchmen. Years later, when he was in the Philadelphia Assembly, he launched a state militia, a hospital, and a university. He also helped to clean, light, and pave city streets.

But Ben was proudest of his library. He understood the importance of an educated, well-read public. Reading encouraged people to think for themselves. "These libraries have improved the general conversation of the Americans and made the common tradesmen and farmers as intelligent as most gentlemen from other countries," he said. Ben also believed that better educated men would fight to protect their rights.

More than forty years later, that is just what Americans would do—in the Revolutionary War.

Chapter Nine
HEALTHY, WEALTHY, AND WISE

When the Library Company was formed in 1732, Franklin was twenty-eight years old. For the next fourteen years, he devoted himself to building up his business and reputation. By the time he was forty-two, he had made enough money to retire from printing and devote himself to his many other interests. It was an astounding accomplishment.

After Ben retired, he tried to keep to a set schedule. His day started early, at 5 A.M. He liked to exercise in the early morning, perhaps going the few short blocks down to the Delaware River for a swim. All his life Franklin believed in fresh air and warm baths. This was unusual in an age in which most people thought frequent baths were unnecessary—and probably unhealthy!

After dressing, he read for an hour or two. Now that he had steady access to new books, he feasted on them. Finally he had the chance to make up for his lack of formal education. He also took the opportunity to learn to read a few foreign languages—French, Italian, and Spanish—as well as polish up his Latin. The "first citizen" of Philadelphia was preparing to be a citizen of the world.

After breakfast, Ben went to his shop at eight o'clock. Like most tradesmen, he lived above his place of work. But by now he had other journeymen printers and apprentices to assist him. At noon he had lunch and read and worked on his accounts. Then, at two, he went back to the shop and worked until six. His evenings were spent conversing with friends and listening to or playing music. For at least an hour, Ben examined his behavior during the day. What good had he accomplished? Then, at ten in the evening, he went to bed.

In all this, at home and at work, Deborah Franklin was her husband's partner. In their early years together, she cooked his meals, wove his clothes, and kept his shop. Franklin was especially proud of her thriftiness. If he could make the money, she could save it.

Sometimes, though, Debby was tempted to spend

money on those she loved. In his autobiography, Franklin remembered that for breakfast they had bread and milk, which Franklin used to eat in a clay bowl with a pewter spoon. One morning she proudly served him in a china bowl with a silver spoon. Her husband, she declared, deserved china and silver as much as their neighbors!

The Franklins had other responsibilities, too. By 1732, Ben had two children. The first, William Franklin, was his son with another woman. No one has ever discovered who she was. William was born in 1731 and came to live with Ben and Debby. They raised him as their own.

In October 1732, the same month that the Library Company received its first shipload of books, Ben and Debby welcomed another son, Francis Franklin. Franklin adored both of his children. And he was devastated when four-year-old Franky came down with smallpox and died. Thirty-six years later he still remembered Franky, "whom to this day I cannot think of without a sigh."

It would be seven long years before Ben and Debby had their next, and last, child, Sally. This time, Franklin made sure his precious daughter was inoculated against smallpox when she was three years old. The Franklins were very proud of Sally. Ben wrote his mother, "Your granddaughter is the greatest lover of her book and school of any child I ever knew."

He made sure Sally had a practical education. She learned reading, writing, arithmetic, and accounting. Like the other young women of her day, Sally had little formal schooling. She grew up to be a warm and affectionate woman who cared for her father in his old age.

~

In the busy Franklin household, with children to support and a business to run, Ben was always on the lookout for new ways to make money. He became the official printer for Pennsylvania. His shop printed all the paper money and official documents for the state. In 1732 he hit upon another scheme that would make him plenty of money—and also make him famous. He created *Poor Richard's Almanack.*

Most households in colonial America had just two books: A Bible and an almanac. Almanacs were a treasure chest of all kinds of useful, amusing, and offbeat information. They contained weather forecasts, calendars, tidal information, planet and star charts, horoscopes, historical anecdotes, proverbs, jokes, poetry, and advice. A new one came out every year, so that a popular almanac could be a source of steady income for a very long time. In *Poor Richard's Almanack*, Franklin had found his gold mine. He would publish it for twenty-five years.

The following advertisement appeared in the *Pennsylvania Gazette*:

> *Just published for 1733: Poor Richard's Almanack containing the lunations, eclipses, planets, motions and aspects, weather, sun and moon's rising and setting, highwater, etc., besides many pleasant and witty verses, jest, and sayings, author's motive of writing...By Richard Saunders, philomath, printed and sold by B. Franklin, price 3s. 6d per dozen.*

The name "Poor Richard" came from the fictional author Franklin invented, named Richard Saunders. Poor Richard was a "philomath," or lover of learning. He wrote the introduction to every volume, chatting to the reader about his fortunes and family life. He offered a store of useful information. But he also had his troubles. Readers felt sorry for Richard because he had little money and a nagging wife. They grew fond of this amusing character with his endless complaints, his money problems, and his marriage woes.

Sometimes the fictitious Richard complained about his printer, the real Ben Franklin. In 1737, for instance, he blamed Franklin for some bad weather predictions. Two years later he groaned that his printer was taking most of his profits. Readers enjoyed the inside joke.

The most famous feature of the almanac, though, was Poor Richard's proverbs. These were sayings used as "fillers" between longer pieces. Most of the sayings were not original. They were old European proverbs that had been passed down for generations. But Franklin rewrote them to make them simpler and easier to remember.

For instance, one old English proverb went, "Fresh fish and new-come guests smell, but that they are three days old." Franklin turned this into the more direct "Fish and visitors stink in three days." "Three may keep a secret if two of them are away" became "Three may keep a secret if two of them are dead."

Poor Richard's sayings have been popular ever since:

He that lies with dogs shall rise up with fleas.
Haste makes waste.
No gains without pains.
God helps those that help themselves.

Little strokes fell great oaks.

Great talkers, little doers.

Don't throw stones if your own windows are made of glass.

A cat in gloves catches no mice.

For want of a nail the shoe is lost; for want of a shoe the horse is lost; for want of a horse the rider is lost.

And perhaps the most famous:

Early to bed and early to rise, makes a man healthy, wealthy, and wise.

In the twenty-five years it was in print, *Poor Richard's Almanack* sold 10,000 copies a year. Printers and booksellers throughout the colonies ordered the almanac directly, ten or eighteen or twenty-five dozen at a time, and sold it to eager customers. It was colonial America's best-selling book, owned by one in every hundred people.

In 1757, Franklin bundled a bunch of Poor Richard's sayings about money and virtue into one book and called it *The Way to Wealth.* In the 1700s, Franklin's book was reprinted in seven languages. In

France it became especially popular as *La Science du Bonhomme Richard*. *The Way to Wealth* is still in print today. In fact, by 2003, the book had been published in more than 1,300 editions!

Franklin found other ways to increase his own wealth. In 1737, he became the Philadelphia postmaster. This meant that his shop was the official post office, and all the news from the other colonies had to be delivered to him first. He not only got the news before other printers, but he could also use the postal riders to deliver his newspaper, so that more people could subscribe to it. Because they knew the *Pennsylvania Gazette* had a wide circulation, more advertisers paid to advertise in its pages. All in all, Franklin said, the job of postmaster "came to afford me a very considerable income."

Franklin also developed a network of printing houses. He would train a new printer, then send him off to a town without a print shop. Franklin would help fund the new business. Then he would receive a third of the profits. Soon he was receiving a steady income from print shops up and down the East Coast.

What did Franklin do with all the money he made? Did he buy a country estate, expensive horses, lots of fancy European clothes?

No. Ben Franklin was never interested in money for its own sake. "I would rather have it said," he once wrote his mother, "'He lived usefully,' than 'He died rich.'" He wanted money for the time it would buy him—time to learn, time to experiment, time to invent. Money, for Franklin, equaled freedom.

In 1748, at the age of forty-two, Ben retired from active business. He turned the day-to-day running of his print shop over to his foreman, David Hall. By the terms of the agreement, Franklin would receive half the shop's profits for the next eighteen years, about £650 a year. That would make him a wealthy man by the standards of the day, when a royal governor earned about £1000, and a mere clerk about £25. Ben would also be receiving a steady income from his printing partnerships, the post office, and real estate investments.

The first thing Franklin did after he retired was to move his household from busy Market Street to a quieter street nearby. There he planned to "read, study, make experiments," and correspond with other learned and ingenious men. He hoped to "produce something for the common benefit of mankind."

One of Poor Richard's sayings offered this advice:

If you would not be forgotten,
As soon as you are dead and rotten,
Either write things worth reading,
Or do things worth the writing.

Ben Franklin planned to do both.

Chapter Ten
THE SPARKS FLY

Throughout his life, Ben Franklin continued to ask questions. Why? How? What? Why does salt dissolve in water? Why are voyages from America to England so much faster than voyages from England to America? How do crabs reproduce? How do ants tell each other where to find food? What causes earthquakes?

Two years before his retirement, Ben had tried to find an answer to the old Junto question, "How can smoky chimneys be cured?" Heating a home in the 1700s was dirty and inefficient. Most colonial fireplaces spewed black smoke into the room. Meanwhile, most of the heat escaped up the chimney.

Franklin designed a stove he hoped would solve these problems. A wood fire in the metal stove would heat the air in an inner metal box. This warm air would then flow out through vents in the side of the stove. But the smoke would be carried out a pipe and up the chimney.

Franklin was very proud of his "Pennsylvania Fireplace." In his advertisements, he claimed that it made the room "twice as warm with a quarter of the wood." He could have made a lot of money from his invention. But he refused to patent it. He wished to serve others "freely and generously," through his inventions.

In order to satisfy his curiosity about the natural world, Franklin dove into every science book the Library Company ordered. He had always been interested in the sciences—in chemistry, mathematics, astronomy, biology. But nothing captured his curiosity the way electricity did.

Not much was known about electricity in the early 1700s. Somehow, people realized, "electrical fire" could be caused by rubbing glass or certain other materials. Sparks would fly out—*hiss, crackle, pop!* And if someone touched the electrified object, he or she could get a small shock—or a big one. Sometimes the jolt would be so great the person would be weak or sore for days.

Traveling showmen used electrical fire to entertain. First they filled a glass container with water, coated it with metal foil, and stopped it up with a cork. A metal rod stuck through the cork was set in the water. This was called a Leyden jar. After the jar was charged with a spark, anyone who touched it would get an electric shock.

In one famous demonstration, a French scientist in Louis XV's court sent a jolt of electricity through 180 soldiers holding hands. As the force passed through them, they all jumped at once. The audience loved it. The king laughed uproariously when the scientist gave the same demonstration with 800 monks.

Franklin had his first opportunity to see the mysterious force in action when he visited Boston in 1743. There a Scottish physician named Dr. Archibald Spencer was thrilling audiences with his electrical demonstrations.

Spencer would rub a long brass tube with his hand, then hold it near pieces of gold leaf. The gold pieces would whirl wildly in the air. Some of them leaped toward the tube—others darted away.

Then, in the climax of the show, Spencer suspended a young boy from the ceiling with silken ropes.

The audience held its breath.

Dr. Spencer rubbed a glass tube near the boy's feet. The boy's hair stood on end. Sparks shot from his face and hands.

Franklin held his knuckles out towards one of the boy's fingers. *Flash!* A spark crackled between them.

Franklin was intrigued. I wish my friends could see this, he thought. He invited Dr. Spencer to come to Philadelphia, and advertised the lectures in the *Gazette.* On May 3, 1744, an announcement read: "A course of experimental philosophy [science] begins in the Library-Room, next Monday at five o'clock in the afternoon."

By 1744, the Library Company had moved to the second floor of Philadelphia's new State House, which later became known as Independence Hall. The rooms housed a collection of more than 400 books and a mini-museum. Thomas Penn's print of an orrery had been the first exhibition. Then came an air-pump from John Penn. Other donors sent fossils, dead animals preserved in glass jars, tanned skins, and all sorts of other strange and interesting objects. The Company owned both a microscope and a telescope, which were often borrowed by scientists.

The Library Company was the perfect place to hold scientific lectures. It was also the perfect place for Franklin to perform his own first experiments in electricity.

Franklin asked the Library's agent in London, Peter

Collinson, to send any information he had on electricity. In 1747, Collinson shipped the Library a long glass tube and instructions for using it. Then Franklin and his friends started their experiments. During the winter of 1748–49, Franklin lived and dreamed electricity.

Oh, how the sparks flew! Franklin and the others rubbed the glass jar and drew sparks from the gilt frames of mirrors or the gilded covers of books. They lit candles and alcohol with electric sparks, and passed electric kisses back and forth between the gentlemen and the ladies.

When they got tired of rubbing the glass by hand, they built a little machine. As they turned the handle, a glass globe spun and rubbed against the pad, glittering merrily away.

Franklin decided to have some fun. He made a little spider of burnt cork, with spindly linen legs. Inside the cork he placed a bit of lead. Then he hung the spider from a bit of silk thread and waited for visitors.

When anyone approached the table—the spider leapt up! The onlookers would jump back, startled. Back and forth the electric spider sprang between an electrified jar on one side of a table and a wire on the other. It looked alive!

Another time, Franklin electrified a painting of King

George II. If someone touched his gilded crown, they got a "high-treason" shock!

Such "electrical amusements" could be really dangerous. Once Franklin himself was nearly electrocuted. He linked two jars together, and touched one of them by mistake. *Flash!* He felt a "universal blow from head to foot throughout the body." His chest was sore for a week afterward. Luckily, Franklin had taken the shock through his hand. If it had come through his head, he realized, he might not still be alive to tell the story.

Playing with electricity was not all fun and games. Franklin made some very important discoveries and invented new ways to describe what he had observed:

⚡ Sometimes objects with an electric charge attracted other objects. Sometimes they pushed them away. Electricity, Franklin decided, must contain equal amounts of *plus* and *minus* charges. Electricity was either *positive* or *negative.*

⚡ Some materials, such as metal or water, carried the electrical charge easily. These were *conductors.* Other materials, such as wax or silk, did not carry the electric charge. They were *insulators.*

⚡ If charged glass and lead plates were wired together, electricity could be stored for later use. These Franklin called electrical *batteries*.

⚡ Electricity was attracted to pointed objects, such as metal rods. This observation would lead to one of Franklin's most famous inventions.

After a winter of electrical amusements, Franklin and his friends decided to have an electrical party. They drank from electrified beakers. They also used an electric shock to kill a turkey for their dinner. The turkey meat, Franklin wrote, was "uncommonly tender."

Franklin sent news of his experiments to Peter Collinson in England. Collinson, in turn, read his letters to the most important scientific organization in England, the Royal Society. Everyone began to speak of this clever American.

Ben thought that what he had learned might help other scientists make still more discoveries. So in 1751 he put the letters together into an eighty-six-page pamphlet and published it. *Experiments and Other Observations on Electricity Made at Philadelphia in America* by Mr. Benjamin Franklin was an immediate hit on both sides of the Atlantic.

Franklin was having the time of his life. Yet he worried that in all his experimentation, he had been able "to discover nothing in the way of use to mankind."

He was about to dream up one of the most useful inventions of all time!

Chapter Eleven
TAMING THE LIGHTNING

Lightning has terrified people since our ancestors first ran for the nearest safe cave. Many interpreted it as a sign of the gods' displeasure. The ancient Greeks thought that Zeus fired lightning bolts down from Mt. Olympus when he was angry. In Europe, people interpreted thunderstorms as a sign from God. They were not considered a natural occurrence—they were *super*-natural.

Most people thought lightning was a kind of fire in the sky. No one had made the connection between electricity and lightning.

As a result, they had no way to defend themselves from lightning strikes. Many people thought that ringing church bells during bad weather would help protect them. When blessed by a priest or minister, bells supposedly had the power to vanquish storms and chase away demons. In reality, bell ringing often seemed to have exactly the opposite effect. In fact, even as the clanging bells sounded across the countryside, lightning sometimes zapped the bell towers and killed the poor ringers.

Why?

The answer, Franklin thought, was simple: lightning and electricity were actually the same thing. In a letter to Collinson, Franklin listed the similarities between them:

1. Giving light.
2. Color of the light.
3. Crooked directions.
4. Swift motion.
5. Conducted by metals.
6. Crack or noise in exploding.
7. Subsisting in water or ice.
8. Rending bodies as it passes through.
9. Destroying animals.
10. Melting metals.
11. Firing inflammable substances.
12. Sulphurous smell.

If lightning was electrical, Franklin reasoned, then ringing church bells was absolutely the worst thing to do during a storm. After all, bells are made of metal, and metal conducts electricity. Also, as Franklin had demonstrated, electricity was attracted by tall, pointy objects—high trees, lofty towers, the masts of ships, and church steeples. A church steeple was not the safest, but the most *dangerous* place to be near during a lightning strike!

There was only one way to find out if Franklin was right. "Let the experiment be made!" he declared.

In *Experiments and Other Observations on Electricity,* Ben described a test he thought would work. This was his plan: Raise an iron rod with a sharp point on top of a high tower or steeple. Fasten the bottom of the rod to a kind of "sentry box" where a man could stand, sheltered from the rain. Then, when lightning flashed across the sky, he could touch the rod with his knuckle or with a wire attached to a wax handle. If he drew sparks, then he would know that the rod was electrified—and that lightning is electricity!

King Louis V of France read about the experiment and was inspired. Why not carry out Monsieur Franklin's ideas in France? At the king's direction, scientists erected a sentry box with a 40-foot iron rod. On

May 10, 1752, a soldier stood in it during a thunderstorm. Lightning cracked across the sky—and sparks shot out of the iron rod! The experiment worked!

In that instant, Benjamin Franklin became world-famous. He had proved that lightning and electricity were one and the same. But he didn't learn right away that his theory had been correct. It took months for word of the French experiments to make its way across the Atlantic.

In the meantime, Franklin came up with another way to prove his theory. Philadelphia contained no buildings tall enough to build a sentry box. What else could he use to carry a metal point into the clouds?

What flew into the sky? Birds, balloons—and kites! That was it! He could use a kite!

Excitedly, Franklin gathered the materials he would need to make his kite. First, a large silk handkerchief. Since silk is stronger than paper, he figured, a silk kite would not rip in the wind.

Next Ben found two cross-sticks to support the silk. He tied each corner of the handkerchief to the ends of the sticks. Then he attached a thin, pointed wire to the upright stick. The wire would extend about a foot above the kite. To the other end of the stick, he attached a long string.

What would keep the electricity from flowing from the metal point down into his hand? Silk, which does not conduct electricity. So at the end of the string, Ben tied a silk ribbon. Finally, between the silk and the string, he tied a metal key. His kite was ready.

Franklin told only his twenty-one-year-old son William what he intended to do. That way, if he was unsuccessful, no one else would ever know.

Restlessly he waited for a thunderstorm. One hot June day, the sky grew black and the wind came up. Franklin and William hurried out to an open field. Franklin stood in the open doorway of a shed, holding tight to the end of the silk ribbon. William ran out into the middle of the field and launched the kite.

Up, up it went, swirling in the gusty wind.

Crack! Lightning flashed across the field. *Boom!* A thunderclap split the sky. Franklin put his knuckle to the key. Would he feel a spark?

Nothing. He tried hard not to be disappointed. How could he have been wrong?

Still he waited, the minutes ticking by. He felt the first cooling drops of rain begin to fall. He glanced at the rope.

What was happening? One by one, the loose threads of the string were standing straight up.

Cautiously he brought his knuckle towards the key. Closer and closer it came...

Zap! A spark shot out into the air.

He'd done it! He'd drawn electricity out of the sky!

Now the rain came pouring down. As Franklin held onto the string, William charged jar after jar with electricity. Franklin would test later to see whether this electricity gathered from the clouds had the same properties as the electricity gathered from the whirling glass globes.

By now the string was soaking wet. The wetter it got, the more easily electricity flowed, and the more William and Ben collected in the Leyden jars. But Franklin knew it was important to keep the silk ribbon dry. If the ribbon got wet, electricity would flow straight down the string into his hand and he would receive another huge electric shock. And *that* shock he might not survive.

Luckily, nothing terrible happened. Ben and his son made it home with all the charged jars. And news of Franklin's achievement soon blazed across America and Europe.

Scientists everywhere tried to copy Franklin's sentry box and kite experiments. In Russia, one poor scientist died when he failed to protect himself properly.

A massive bolt flashed right through his body, electrocuting him.

Now Franklin had to figure out a way to make his discovery useful. He came up with a wonderful idea.

He would invent a way to protect buildings from lightning!

Franklin proposed that long metal rods be attached to the highest parts of buildings and down their sides into the ground. Then, when clouds became electrified during a storm, the electricity would be drawn out of the air and down the wire and be "grounded" into the earth. The building would be saved.

Franklin had invented the lightning rod! That summer, he put a lightning rod on his own house and on the State House in Philadelphia. This way the books of the Library Company would be safe during storms.

Slowly but surely, lightning rods were placed on buildings across Europe and America. Thousands of buildings were saved from destruction. The bell tower at St. Mark's in Venice, for instance, was blasted by lightning eight times between 1388 and 1761. After being fitted with a lightning rod, it was never damaged by lightning again!

Once again, Franklin refused to patent his invention. He wanted all humanity to benefit from it. In *Poor*

Richard's Almanack for 1753, he published directions for constructing a lightning rod. If people installed the rods, he wrote, they would be safe from "the most sudden and terrible mischief."

The world was grateful. And the awards began to pile up. Franklin received the prestigious gold Copley Medal from London's Royal Society for scientific achievement. The King of France sent him his personal "compliments." In America, Harvard and Yale Universities both awarded him honorary degrees. Years later, so did Oxford University in England and the University of St. Andrews in Scotland. From then on, the scholars of St. Andrews said, Benjamin Franklin should be called "the worthy Doctor." So to the end of his life, Franklin—who had never gone to college—was known as "Dr. Franklin."

Chapter Twelve
A TIME OF CHANGE

At age forty-seven, Benjamin Franklin had come a long way from the bedraggled runaway who had slipped into Philadelphia thirty years before. Now he was wealthy, respected, and world-famous.

He could never have been such a success without his books. Because of his hunger for knowledge, he had become the best writer and printer in the colonies and one of the leading scientists in the world. Other ambitious young men, he thought, should have access to books and learning. But they shouldn't have to find their own books the way he had. Franklin knew that most boys did not have his special intelligence and drive. No, there was an easier way. They could go to college.

The thirteen colonies already had four colleges: Harvard in Boston, Massachusetts; William and Mary in Williamsburg, Virginia; Yale in New Haven, Connecticut; and Princeton in Princeton, New Jersey. It was time for Philadelphia to have a college of its own.

Franklin gained support for his idea in the Junto and wrote a pamphlet advertising the plan. He wanted to create a college where young men would learn to be good citizens. The "great aim and end of all learning," Franklin said, should be to "serve mankind, one's country, friends, and family." The new academy would stress practical knowledge: science, mathematics, history, accounting, business, and writing. And in an age when most European colleges taught Greek and Latin, Franklin planned to offer a good education in the English language.

Once he had the support he needed, he quickly raised £2,000 in donations, found a hall, and hired an administrator. In January 1751, the academy opened, with more than a hundred male scholars. (In the 1700s, no one thought seriously about higher education for women. Oberlin, the first co-ed American college, didn't open until 1833.) The Pennsylvania Academy, later known as the University of Pennsylvania, was born.

By the 1750s, Philadelphia was the largest city in the thirteen colonies. The colonial population shot up during the first half of the 1700s, from about 300,000 in 1700 to 1,485,000 in 1750. More farmers produced more wheat and tobacco; more fishermen caught more cod and mackerel; more craftsmen made more candles, barrels, furniture, and ships. As the coastal towns grew crowded, settlers pushed further west, where land was plentiful. It was a time of expansion and growing prosperity.

The Library Company grew, too, during these years. For a while, in the 1740s, Franklin acted as secretary. But he was a messy record keeper. The secretary who took over later found that Franklin had taken notes on many separate pieces of paper. Some of them were lost, never to be found again. He was still having trouble trying to be neat and orderly!

Throughout the 1750s, boxes of books continued to arrive and be catalogued. So did curiosities from all over the globe: a collection of Roman coins, Eskimo parkas and tools, and even the mummified hand of an Egyptian princess. Membership kept growing as well. In 1769, the first woman was voted in as a shareholder of the Library Company.

As Philadelphia and the Library grew, so did the range of Franklin's interests and responsibilities. In 1751 he became a member of the Pennsylvania Assembly. As the most influential person in the

Assembly, he was chosen in 1757 to go to England to represent the colony's interests there. Franklin wanted to defend Pennsylvania against the heirs of founder William Penn. The Penns drained too much money from the colony, colonists felt, and didn't pay taxes to support it.

Franklin thought that colonists had the same rights as other British subjects. He was shocked to discover that most Englishmen regarded Americans as second-class citizens. Although Franklin still considered himself a loyal subject of the crown, he understood for the first time that the colonies had no power.

It turned out that Franklin would spend fifteen of the seventeen years between 1757 and 1775 in London. Deborah did not go with him to England. She refused ever to leave Philadelphia; she would not even travel as far as Boston. She was afraid of the dangerous ocean voyage. Ben wrote Deborah many letters, but he wasn't there when she grew old and sick. Deborah died on December 19, 1774, four months before he came home.

During the last ten years Franklin was in England, he tried to work out a compromise between the angry colonies and the mother country. In these years, England demanded taxes from the colonies that they did not want to pay. The thirteen colonies had no representatives in Parliament to stand up for American interests, the colonists argued. This was taxation without representation!

In the midst of the political conflicts, Franklin decided to write his own book. All his life, Franklin had only written short pieces of prose. He was a journalist, after all. Even *The Way to Wealth* and *Experiments and Other Observations in Electricity* were put together from shorter articles and letters.

But in 1771, at the age of sixty-five, Franklin thought it was time to try to write his life story. Other people, he thought, would be interested in learning how he achieved his wealth and fame. He began the book by pretending he was writing to his son William. While he was in England, he completed the chapters up to the time when he started the Library Company.

But Franklin could not finish his autobiography. Too many important things were happening. The colonies had become even more angry with England. They refused to pay unfair British taxes, especially the tax on tea. On December 16, 1773, a group of men and boys disguised as Mohawk Indians sneaked onto a ship in Boston Harbor and dumped chests of tea into the harbor.

The Boston Tea Party, as it was called, enraged the

British. They closed down the port of Boston and placed the city under the control of British soldiers. Throughout the colonies, people rallied in support of Boston.

In the meantime, Franklin still worked for peace. But finally even Franklin realized that his usefulness in London was at an end. In March 1775, he sailed for home. A month later, violence broke out at Lexington and Concord in Massachusetts. America and Britain were at war.

~

Not long after Franklin returned to Pennsylvania, a meeting of all the colonies was called. This came to be known as the First Continental Congress. Franklin was chosen as a delegate. The Congress needed a place to meet.

When Franklin's Library Company had grown to over 2,000 books, the members had realized they needed more room. In 1773, they had moved to larger quarters in the new Carpenter's Hall. The library invited all the delegates to use it for the meeting. In that way, the Library Company became the first library of the first government of the future United States.

Only one library slip from that time has ever been found. One delegate took out a copy of Thomas Paine's *Common Sense.* Paine was a writer who called for American independence from Britain. As Franklin had hoped, the Library Company remained a center for the free exchange of ideas during the Revolution.

Even though they were fighting a war, for a long time the delegates to the First Continental Congress were reluctant to take the last step and declare independence from England. Finally they formed a committee to write a Declaration of Independence. It was made up of Thomas Jefferson, John Adams, Roger Sherman, Robert Livingston—and Benjamin Franklin.

The brilliant thirty-two-year-old Jefferson wrote the first draft. He drew on the English philosopher John Locke's ideas about liberty. People have certain natural, God-given rights, Jefferson wrote, including "life, liberty, and the pursuit of happiness." Great Britain had tried to take away these basic rights. Now the American people had the right to change their government—and revolt.

Franklin helped to edit the final version. The Continental Congress adopted the Declaration of Independence on July 4, 1776. When the document was signed, Franklin turned to the others and said,

"Gentlemen, we must now all hang together, or we shall most assuredly hang separately." Franklin and the others knew that what they had just done was considered by English law to be treason, a crime punishable by death. They had indeed just pledged "our lives, our fortunes and our sacred honor."

The Declaration of Independence was printed at Franklin's old print shop. Then it was published for all of America—and the world—to read.

Chapter Thirteen
THE FIRST AMERICAN

On May 28, 1787, people strolling along Market Street saw a peculiar sight. Four prisoners from the local jail walked slowly down the street. Across their shoulders they carried a sedan chair on two long poles. On the chair sat an old man with flowing white hair and gold spectacles. It was the eighty-one-year-old Benjamin Franklin.

Ben was now so frail that he could not walk even the block from his house to the State House. Yet it was extremely important that he make this short journey. Inside the State House was gathered the most important assembly in American history—the Constitutional Convention.

Eleven years had passed since Franklin had signed the Declaration of Independence in that very same building. During that time the colonists had fought and won the Revolutionary War against Great Britain. Under the leadership of General George Washington, the upstart Americans had beaten the most powerful army in the world.

Franklin spent the war years in Paris. It was his task to convince the French to side with the American colonists against the British. The French adored the man they called Bonhomme Richard (their name for Poor Richard). Franklin coaxed and flattered, begged and bargained. In 1778 the French decided to support the Americans. They sent soldiers and a fleet of ships.

Franklin remained in France, working for the American cause. He was still there when the war officially ended, eight years after it had begun. On September 3, 1783, Franklin and two other American delegates signed the Treaty of Paris, establishing peace with Great Britain. Franklin, now a very old man, had performed an invaluable service. Finally it was time to come home.

In 1787, he was comfortably settled in his Market Street house, surrounded by family—his daughter Sally and her husband, his many grandchildren, and friends. He held court under the mulberry tree in his garden. There he entertained George Washington, James

Madison, Alexander Hamilton and many others. And there he read many of the eighteen boxes of books he brought back from France.

The man who had always hungered for more books now had one of the largest collections—perhaps the largest—in the United States. To hold them, he built himself a magnificent new library. It took up the whole second floor of his house and was filled with shelves from floor to ceiling. When he found he couldn't reach the books on the top shelves, Franklin invented a "long, artificial arm and hand" to take them down.

In addition to 4,276 books, the library contained Franklin's electrical equipment and other scientific instruments. One glass machine showed the circulation of blood in the human body. It also held some of Franklin's inventions. One of them was a rocker with a built-in fan. To feel a soft cooling breeze, all he had to do was press a pedal with his foot.

Franklin admitted to his sister Jane that it was probably foolish for him to build a grand library at such an advanced age. "But we are apt to forget that we are grown old," he explained. "And building is such an amusement." Books were, as they had been all his life, his greatest enjoyment. Not willing to waste a moment, he even read in the bath. He had a long copper tub, shaped like a shoe. Franklin's legs slid under the "tongue," to which he attached a book rest.

All during the hot summer months of 1787, delegates to the Constitutional Convention met behind closed doors to draw up a blueprint for the new nation. The proceedings were so secret that even the windows were closed.

Despite the intense heat and humidity, Benjamin Franklin never missed a session. He was by far the oldest delegate there. He was also the best traveled, the most knowledgeable, and the most famous, with the possible exception of George Washington. Other delegates were eager to hear what he had to say.

He did not say much. Franklin was not a sparkling public speaker. Besides, he was too weak to stand for long. James Wilson, another Pennsylvania delegate, usually read his remarks for him.

Even so, Franklin had great influence on the Convention. It was split on many issues: How long should the President serve? How many representatives should each state have in Congress? What should the new nation do about slavery?

Whatever the issue, Franklin always counseled compromise. "Both sides must part with some of their demands," he insisted. Only if they found common ground would the great "experiment" of democracy work.

Finally compromise after compromise had been hammered out. The Constitution was ready for signing. It was then that Franklin delivered his final advice. No human being, and no human endeavor, he said, could be perfect. But the Constitution came as close as any manmade creation could get. "I consent, Sir, to this Constitution because I expect no better," he wrote, "and because I am not sure that it is not the best."

He urged all the delegates to sign the new Constitution. Most of them did. When Franklin's speech was published for the American people to read, it helped them accept their new form of government.

The long story of Franklin's life was nearly over. As he retreated to his garden, Franklin thought about the past eighty years. He had had a happy life, he wrote a friend. "If I were allowed to live it over again, I should make no objection, only wishing to do what authors do in a second edition of their works, correct some of my errata [errors]."

He lived long enough to dedicate the cornerstone of the new Library Company in 1789. Over the doorway would stand a statue of Franklin in classical robes. But Franklin did not see the library completed. He died in 1790, at the age of eighty-four.

The day of Franklin's funeral, a crowd of 20,000 people filled Philadelphia's streets. He was buried next to Deborah under a plain marble tombstone in the cemetery at Christ Church. The tombstone said simply: "Benjamin and Deborah Franklin 1790."

At age twenty-two, Ben had written his own epitaph. It compared his life to a book. It turned out that the epitaph was not engraved upon his tombstone when he died. But perhaps it should have been:

The Body of
B. Franklin, Printer;
(Like the Cover of an old Book,
Its Contents torn out
And stript of its Lettering and Gilding)
Lies here, Food for Worms,
But the Work shall not be lost;
For it will, (as he believ'd) appear once more,
In a new and more elegant Edition
Revised and corrected,
By the Author.

The Amazing

Mr. Franklin

Benjamin Franklin lived in very exciting times—and helped make them even more exciting!

Here are just a few of the many roles he played throughout his life:

Mr. Franklin, Patriot

Benjamin Franklin lived for almost an entire century, from 1706 to 1790. The year he was born, about 330,000 people lived in eleven English colonies on the shores of the Atlantic Ocean.

The year Franklin died, there were 3,929,000 people living in thirteen states.

When Franklin was born, colonists thought of themselves as British citizens and loyal subjects of the king.

By the time Franklin died, they thought of themselves as Americans.

Franklin was one of the first to suggest that the thirteen colonies unite for the common good. In 1754, in the middle of the French and Indian War, settlers in the west were under

FIRST POLITICAL CARTOON

constant attack from raiding Indians. British troops were not doing a very good job of protecting them. Franklin suggested that the colonies come together to form a continental militia. To make his point, he drew the first political cartoon in America. It showed a snake chopped up in eight little pieces. The cartoon warned: "Join or Die!"

Twenty-two years later, the colonies did unite. They shocked the world by rebelling against the mightiest nation on earth, Great Britain. And Franklin, perhaps the most famous American, was one of the chief rebels.

Benjamin Franklin was the only Founding Father to sign all three important documents of the American Revolution: the Declaration of Independence, the peace treaty with Britain, and the Constitution.

In some ways, Franklin was a lot like the new nation. He was bold, inventive, practical, and hard-working. He was self-made, and proud of it. Above all, Franklin believed in freedom: freedom of speech, freedom of religion, freedom of conscience. He believed that every citizen should have the chance, through hard work and talent, to make it on his own. No wonder Benjamin Franklin is sometimes called the "First American."

Mr. Franklin, Scientist

During the 1700s, scientists proposed bold theories about the laws of nature. Then they performed experiments to test them. Always curious, Franklin kept up with the

latest science news. He made amazing discoveries, too. He invented mostly useful—and sometimes quite unusual—things.

The Franklin stove and the lightning rod are probably his most famous inventions. But there were many more,

THE FRANKLIN STOVE

including:

Bifocals—As Franklin got older, he found he needed two pairs of glasses—one for seeing objects far away and another for reading. He

BEN'S "DOUBLE SPECTACLES"

found it troublesome to have to switch between them. So he asked a glassmaker to cut both sets of glasses in half and reset them into wire frames. The far-

sighted glass went on the top. The nearsighted glass went on the bottom. That way, Franklin wrote, "I have only to move my eyes up or down, as I want to see distinctly far or near." He called his new glasses "double spectacles."

**BEN PLAYING HIS
GLASS ARMONICA**

BEN'S FIRST GLASS ARMONICA DESIGN

Glass armonica—This was a new musical instrument, made of 37 glass bowls of different sizes. Franklin nested the bowls together and placed them on a glass rod. The performer would make the glass spin by pressing a foot pedal. When she touched the spinning glass, beautiful, pure tones were created. For a while, the glass armonica was very popular. Famous musicians like Mozart and Beethoven composed for Franklin's instrument.

Here are some of Franklin's scientific discoveries:

Lead poisoning. Ben noticed that craftsmen—such as glassmakers, plumbers, and painters—who worked with certain metals became ill with "dry belly ache." What did these craftsmen have in common? They all worked with lead! Franklin warned the craftsmen of the danger.

The reason for colds. Franklin noticed that people seemed to "catch cold from one another" in closed rooms and carriages. Perhaps the air carried the illness? Franklin didn't use the word "germs" to describe what the air carried. Germs hadn't been discovered yet. But Franklin was on the right track. All his life, he insisted on fresh air and open windows.

Daylight savings time. Franklin was the first to propose that people get up earlier in the summer to save money on candles.

Mr. Franklin, Book-Lover

When Franklin founded the Library Company, he started a new idea: creating libraries that *everyone* could use, not just scholars and the very wealthy. In 1854, The Boston Public Library opened. It was the first free public library supported by taxes instead of private donations. At the end of the 1800s, steel magnate Andrew Carnegie gave $50 million to build more free libraries. There are now 1,946 Carnegie libraries in the United States.

The Library Company of Philadelphia still exists. In 2004,

LIBRARY COMPANY OF PHILADELPHIA'S FIFTH STREET ENTRANCE, C.1800

it was 273 years old! The library contains an important collection of books and other research materials about American history and culture up to the year 1900.

Franklin knew how important libraries would be in a democracy. Reading gives citizens the education and knowledge to decide issues for themselves. No wonder nine signers of the Declaration of Independence were members of the Library Company!

Mr. Franklin, Autobiographer

Benjamin Franklin is the author of the most popular autobiography ever written. He didn't start writing the story of his life until he was 65 years old. Because he was such a busy man, he stopped and started again four times between 1771 and 1790. Unfortunately, he died before it was completed. As a result, the *Autobiography* ends before the American Revolution even starts!

People love the *Autobiography* anyway. Ben Franklin's rise from rags to riches is often called the American Dream. Franklin lived that dream. And so, he insisted, can anyone else!

Mr. Franklin and His Family

After 1755, Ben Franklin lived most of his life in Europe. He kept in touch with his family by writing many letters and sending gifts. His daughter Sally grew up to marry a shopkeeper named Richard Bache. The couple had seven children. Sally and Richard also cared for Franklin in his old age.

DAUGHTER SARAH, KNOWN AS SALLY

The story of Franklin's son William is very sad. For many years, William lived with his father in England. In 1762, he became royal governor of New Jersey. When the Revolution broke out, he sided with England—against his own father.

William's loyalty to the British king made Ben Franklin very angry. After the war was

SON WILLIAM

over, William wrote his father and tried to make up. Franklin refused. William was heartbroken.

Franklin was close to two of his grandsons. He took William's son Temple Franklin with him when he went to Paris in 1776. Temple, alas, grew up to be a ne'er-do-well who did not accomplish much. But Franklin would never admit his grandson's faults.

Sally's six-year-old son Benjamin Franklin Bache also traveled with his grandfather. With Franklin, young Benny was thrilled

GRANDSON TEMPLE

to watch the world's first hot-air balloon flights near Paris. As an adult, Benny followed his grandfather into the printing business. He was a fiery newspaper editor and fighter for civil liberties. All his life, Franklin remained his hero.

MONTGOLFIER BROTHERS' HOT AIR BALLOON. ON SEPTEMBER 19, 1783, FIRST LIVE PASSENGERS WERE A SHEEP, A DUCK, AND A ROOSTER .

Bibliography

Brands, H. W. *The First American: The Life and Times of Benjamin Franklin*. New York: Doubleday, 2000.

Bowen, Catherine Drinker. *The Most Dangerous Man in America*. Boston: Little Brown, 1974.

Cohen, I. Bernard. *Benjamin Franklin's Science*. Cambridge: Harvard University Press, 1990.

Dibner, Bern. *Benjamin Franklin, Electrician*. Norwalk, CT: Burndy Library, 1976.

Green, James. "Subscription Libraries and Commercial Circulating Libaries."

Isaacson, Walter. *Benjamin Franklin: An American Life*. New York: Simon and Schuster, 2003.

Lemay, J. A. Leo, and P. M. Zall, eds. *Benjamin Franklin's Autobiography: An Authoritative Text, Backgrounds, Criticism*. New York: Norton, 1986.

Lopez, Claude-Anne. and Eugenia W. Herbert. *The Private Franklin*. New York: Norton, 1975.

Van Doren, Carl. *Benjamin Franklin*. New York: Viking, 1938.

Wolf, Edwin. *"At the Instance of Benjamin Franklin." A Brief History of the Library Company of Philadelphia, 1731–1976*. Philadelphia: The Library Company, 1976.

Wright, Esmond. *Benjamin Franklin: His Life as He Wrote It*. Cambridge, MA: Harvard University Press, 1990.

Wroth, Lawrence C. *The Colonial Printer*. New York: Dover, 1994.

For Further Reading

Adler, David. *B. Franklin, Printer*. New York: Holiday House, 2001.

Fleming, Candace. *Ben Franklin's Almanac: Being a True Account of the Good Gentleman's Life*. New York: Atheneum, 2003.

Fradin, Dennis. *Who Was Benjamin Franklin?* New York: Grosset & Dunlap, 2002.

Giblin, James Cross. *The Amazing Life of Benjamin Franklin*. New York: Scholastic, 2000.

Rudy, Lisa Jo, ed. *The Ben Franklin Book of Easy and Incredible Experiments: A Franklin Institute Science Museum Book*, New York: John Wiley, 1995.

About the Author

Ruth Ashby has written many award-winning biographies and nonfiction books for children, including *Herstory*, *The Elizabethan Age*, and *Pteranodon: Story of a Pterosaur*. She lives on Long Island, NY with her husband, daughter, and dog, Nubby.